I0687736

Palestine, New Mexico

by Richard Montoya

A SAMUEL FRENCH ACTING EDITION

SAMUEL FRENCH

FOUNDED 1830

NEW YORK HOLLYWOOD LONDON TORONTO

SAMUELFRENCH.COM

Copyright © 2010 by Richard Montoya

ALL RIGHTS RESERVED

Cover design by Richard Montoya and Brandon Oaks

CAUTION: Professionals and amateurs are hereby warned that *PALES-TINE, NEW MEXICO* is subject to a Licensing Fee. It is fully protected under the copyright laws of the United States of America, the British Commonwealth, including Canada, and all other countries of the Copyright Union. All rights, including professional, amateur, motion picture, recitation, lecturing, public reading, radio broadcasting, television and the rights of translation into foreign languages are strictly reserved. In its present form the play is dedicated to the reading public only.

The amateur live stage performance rights to *PALESTINE, NEW MEXICO* are controlled exclusively by Samuel French, Inc., and licensing arrangements and performance licenses must be secured well in advance of presentation. PLEASE NOTE that amateur Licensing Fees are set upon application in accordance with your producing circumstances. When applying for a licensing quotation and a performance license please give us the number of performances intended, dates of production, your seating capacity and admission fee. Licensing Fees are payable one week before the opening performance of the play to Samuel French, Inc., at 45 W. 25th Street, New York, NY 10010.

Licensing Fee of the required amount must be paid whether the play is presented for charity or gain and whether or not admission is charged.

Stock licensing fees quoted upon application to Samuel French, Inc.

For all other rights than those stipulated above, apply to: Samuel French, Inc., 45 West 25th Street, New York, NY 10010.

Particular emphasis is laid on the question of amateur or professional readings, permission and terms for which must be secured in writing from Samuel French, Inc.

Copying from this book in whole or in part is strictly forbidden by law, and the right of performance is not transferable.

Whenever the play is produced the following notice must appear on all programs, printing and advertising for the play: "Produced by special arrangement with Samuel French, Inc."

Due authorship credit must be given on all programs, printing and advertising for the play.

ISBN 978-0-573-69838-5   Printed in U.S.A.   #29640

No one shall commit or authorize any act or omission by which the copyright of, or the right to copyright, this play may be impaired.

No one shall make any changes in this play for the purpose of production.

Publication of this play does not imply availability for performance. Both amateurs and professionals considering a production are strongly advised in their own interests to apply to Samuel French, Inc., for written permission before starting rehearsals, advertising, or booking a theatre.

No part of this book may be reproduced, stored in a retrieval system, or transmitted in any form, by any means, now known or yet to be invented, including mechanical, electronic, photocopying, recording, videotaping, or otherwise, without the prior written permission of the publisher.

MUSIC USE NOTE

Licensees are solely responsible for obtaining formal written permission from copyright owners to use copyrighted music in the performance of this play and are strongly cautioned to do so. If no such permission is obtained by the licensee, then the licensee must use only original music that the licensee owns and controls. Licensees are solely responsible and liable for all music clearances and shall indemnify the copyright owners of the play and their licensing agent, Samuel French, Inc., against any costs, expenses, losses and liabilities arising from the use of music by licensees.

**IMPORTANT BILLING AND CREDIT
REQUIREMENTS**

All producers of *PALESTINE, NEW MEXICO must* give credit to the Author of the Play in all programs distributed in connection with performances of the Play, and in all instances in which the title of the Play appears for the purposes of advertising, publicizing or otherwise exploiting the Play and/ or a production. The name of the Author *must* appear on a separate line on which no other name appears, immediately following the title and *must* appear in size of type not less than fifty percent of the size of the title type.

In addition the following credit *must* be given on all title pages in all programs:

Originally Commissioned by the Circuit Network

PALESTINE, NEW MEXICO was first produced in the Center Theatre Group's Mark Taper Forum on December 13, 2009. The performance was directed by Lisa Peterson, with sets by Rachel Hauck, costumes by Christopher Acebo, lighting design and projections by Alexander Nichols, and sound by Paul James Prendergast. The production stage manager was Susie Walsh. The cast was as follows:

CAPT. CATHERINE SILER	Kirsten Potter
BRONSON	Ric Salinas
TOP HAT	Richard Montoya
FARMER	Herbert Siguenza
MARIA 15	Geraldine Keams
CHIEF BIRDSONG	Russell Means
DACOTAH, GIRL IN BLUE DRESS	Julia Jones
GHOST OF BIRDSONG, SUAREZ	Justin Rain

CHARACTERS

Captain Siler
Bronson
Top Hat
Farmer
Maria 15
Chief Birdsong
Dacotah
Girl in Blue Dress
Ghost of Birdsong
Suarez
Starman
Bog Mountain
Broke Arrow
Sally 30/30
LA Megadeath

Please note: Some characters may be doubled.

AUTHOR'S NOTES

I will never ever forget Lisa Kron, the stellar playwright/actor, for teaching me the Kaddish word for word in the lobby of the Mark Taper Forum. This was my 'Hebrew School' and it would have been sort of cute except that it was so darn important, important to Lisa and her collaborator Leigh Silverman that I get it right. I too felt a jolt of responsibility not to tread on the Kaddish as I would not on sacred Navajo burial songs or the Rosary for that matter. I was touched that Lisa spent so much time and wanted me to get it right. That hour in the lobby felt like 10 years of Yeshiva!

I have to thank Artistic Director Michael Ritchie for allowing us to do PNM as such a production level. Rachel Hauck's set was our Rushmore and I give her and video artist Alex Nichol's and sound guru PJP special thanks along with LP, JG & CC. And a stage crew that is the best in the nation: IATSIE Local 33: Bob Ruby, Howie, Bubba, Bones, Billie and Dana. Thanks too to Riki Lurie and Brandon Oaks for help on the book cover and the Great Russell Means and his essential Pearl for the New Mexican green chili! A-ho!

-Richard Montoya

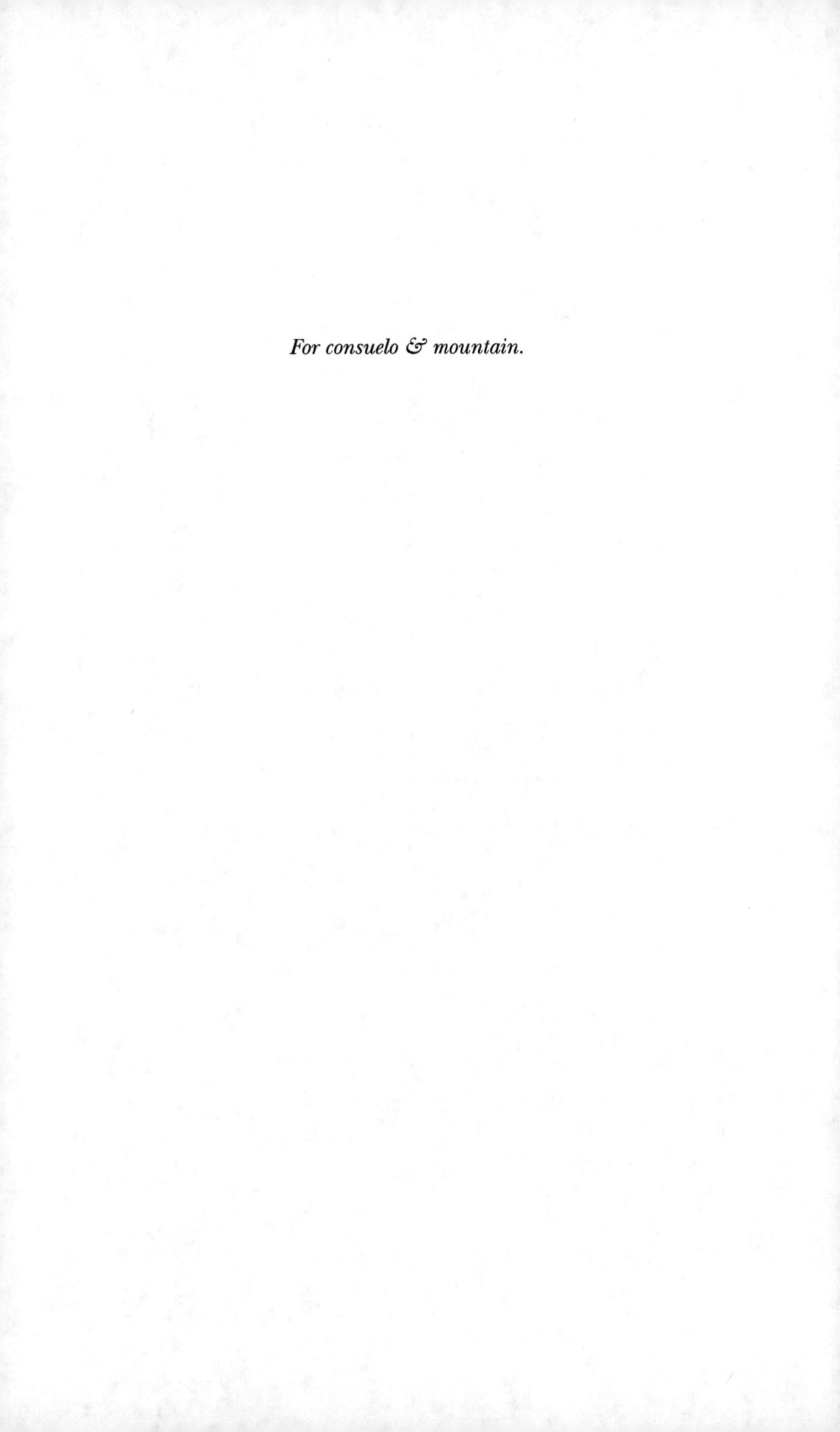

For consuelo & mountain.

CHAPTER 1:
Somebody in the Desert

(A desert landscape swiftly grows dark and cobalt blue.

A Muslim Call to Prayer is heard.

Distant rocket fire and flashes dot the horizon.

A sliver of a crescent moon slowly appears.

In the darkness **TWO PEOPLE** *move into position.*

SOMEBODY *is talking to* **SOMEONE.**

Both are hunched over a small fire. Duffle bag.

There is an animal quality: crouched, yet ready to strike.
The Muslim Call to Prayer subsides under:)

SOMEBODY. So, in that courtyard Soldier, next to the bazaar, this courtyard…

(pointing down to a square she drew in the dirt)

SOMEBODY. Here. There was no code. No rules. No faith. No Tribes. No Hellfire missile cover. No Apache gun ships. No Gods…

(Distant thunder or gunfire. The second person is listening, a shrug or a nod but not speaking.)

SOMEBODY. Trust no one. Believe nothing. No family. No Army. No country in that courtyard. Scorched earth. But, there was you: Private First Class Raymond Birdsong. Why?

(Distant walky-talky snippets. Lights shift subtle.)

SOMEBODY. I was waiting with Echo Company near the Sector, where you should have been.

(SOMEONE stands.)

SOMEBODY. What were you doing there in the courtyard? Answer your Captain, soldier. I will find out.

(**SOMEONE** *takes a few steps away.*)

SOMEBODY. Tried tracking you back to Dover but I lost you. Second time inside a month I lose you.

I'm hungry. What'chu got? MORE. Gimmie.

(**SOMEONE** *tosses a small plastic bag.*)

SOMEBODY. Oh. Tuna ambrosia. Yum. Taste like shit.

(*She tosses it back.*)

SOMEBODY. What the hell happened to you?

(*Echo. Distant animal howls echo thru the dessert.*)

(**SOMEBODY** *is U.S. Army Captain Catherine* **SILER.**)

(**SOMEONE** *is a Soldier: Raymond* **BIRDSONG***: Deceased.*)

SILER. No-sleep mode for seven days now.

Army doc cut off all my meds, just cut em' off.

(**SILER** *tries to drink from an empty canteen.*)

Dry mouth, fighting forgetfulness and thoughts of suicide. Fuck it.

These colors don't run, dude. Work real hard to keep all my soldiers alive, get them all home. But this little Indian here, you Ray, you went off the reservation and you got away and I needed those med's for the last flight out of Ramstein…

(*Other shadowy* **FIGURES** *begin to appear on the ridge above* **CAPTAIN SILER.** **BIRDSONG** *slips away.*)

Last flight out of Ramstein, I stood in the hold of a C Transport *and* 32 coffins 32 flags draped over each aluminum box.

Formaldehyde and the rattle of our sacred cargo. Engines roar, flags over metal boxes. I did not feel a thing. Could not feel. Would not feel.

I was nothing in the void of flag draped coffins.

(**SILER** *pushes down confusion and pain.*)

SILER. *(cont.)* I gotta bring this kid in.

Where the fuck am I? Which Desert of Death am I in? Rigestan? Khost? Ghazni? The Gates if Sau? No. Yeah. Wait. I'm in the middle of Bumbfuck…

(More people enter the ridge above **SILER**.*)*

Bumbfuck, New Mexico. *This* desert…

(In an instant lights up to reveal armed **INDIAN MEN** *and* **WOMEN** *on the ridge above her, some of the men wear versions of cowboy hats with feathers. Sound: wind, deep drums. Rifles. Chains. Bats. Hatchets are all aimed at* **SILER**.*)*

CHAPTER 2:
Siler and the Ridge

(A Wheelchair Indian has joined the ridge posse.)

(A severe Native-American man named **BRONSON** *speaks.)*

BRONSON. You are on Indian Land.
You have illegally entered the private property of a sovereign nation. The men standing here are authorized under US *and* Indian law to shoot any and all trespassers.

SILER. You have a very big gun. Sir.

BRONSON. Big man requires big gun.

SILER. Is that a Bush Master?

BRONSON. That is a fact jack. Almost took you down with her.

SILER. Who's in charge here?

BRONSON. You *need* to get the fuck on down the road, lady. Pardon my French nobody welcomes you here.

SILER. One of *your* men let me pass thru the main gate.

BRONSON. One of *my* men let you on *my* rez?

SILER. Could I get some water please?

BRONSON. What fucking genius would have let you on the rez? Had to be Farmer! Fucking Farmer…

RIDGE MEN. Farmer…Yep…figures…Indian Shreck.

BRONSON. I thought we furloughed his ass due to budget cuts.

BROKE ARROW. He's back.

BRONSON. Track him down then. Pronto!

SILER. Sir, I need to see the Chief, Raymond's father. Are you the Chief?

(The **MEN** *on the ridge chuckle.)*

BRONSON. I am not the Chief. But I am an extremely important man to the Chief.

SILER. Naturally I assumed you were the Chief.

BRONSON. When you assume, soldier, you make an ass out of you and me. The Chief protects the tribe, I protect the Chief. He's my bailiwick.

SILER. Yes sir.

BRONSON. Right now the Chief isn't receiving anybody in his hour. Especially a Fed from the U.S. fucking Army.

SILER. Sir.

BRONSON. We're preparing to bury his boy at sunrise.

SILER. Sunrise?

BRONSON. This is an extremely sacred ceremony. Strictly tribal family only. Understood?

SILER. I'm Captain Catherine Siler. US Army. 21st Military Police Company.

BRONSON. Whoa, whoah, the 21st Company?

MOUNTAIN. Same as our Ray Ray…

SILER. The very same as Private First Class Raymond Birdsong. Yes, sir.

(murmurs from the **MEN** *)*

May I ask your name, sir?

BRONSON. They call me Bronson. Like the great one-fourth Native-American actor.

SILER. Ray served under my command in Afghanistan.

BRONSON. *(bowed head)* Where he died.

SILER. Yes, sir.

BRONSON. You still need to be on the other side of the rez wire. Go on git now.

SILER. Not 'til I speak with the Chief.

BRONSON. You have no privileges here Captain.

SILER. I could really use a drink of water, please.

(only silence as the **MEN** *do not budge)*

Look man, Bronson, dude, I've been driving 36 hours non-stop, half out of my mind so excuse me. Landed in Fort Benning day before last.

BRONSON. *(quietly)* Fuck Georgia.

SILER. I came directly here to speak with the Chief. He needs to know Ray's Captain is here.

BRONSON. You don't give orders here, Captain.

STAR MAN. How come the Army didn't bring you into Fort Bliss? Texas is real close ya know.

(**STAR MAN** *tosses the duffle at her feet.*)

SILER. Sometimes the Army has its head up its ass.

(*The* **MEN** *like this.*)

Whole lotta guns on the rez. Show a gun. Use a gun.

BRONSON. We have to be armed at all times.

SILER. Why?

TOP HAT. I can answer that! That's my area, Bronson.

(*Just then an Indian wearing a* **TOP HAT** *riding a tricked out Stingray bike swoops down. This is:* **TOP HAT**.)

Back up Star Man, Take it easy everybody. Move Aside.

(*He parks and de-bikes.*)

Easy, Trigger.

(*To bike – he then turns his gaze to* **CAPTAIN SILER**.)

Why? (*scolding himself*) Damn. How. I'm the Information Officer around these parts, ma'am. You can call me Top Hat. This is known as the El Paso Corridor. And you can bet your Narco-Traficantes, the Mexican Cartels like to run their heroin & crystal meth, weapons and humans right thru the *mesa* yonder there.

STAR MAN. Armed Coyotes smuggle the Wets through the Rio Grande less than a mile away.

SILER. Damn good reasons to be armed.

STAR MAN, MOUNTAIN & BROKE ARROW. (*smile*) Thank *you.*

TOP HAT. The Halliburton assholes are building their new border fence just south – there.

BROKE ARROW. Shovel ready stimulus project.

MOUNTAIN. I'm going to take a piss on that Fuckin Lou Dobbs memorial wall…

TOP HAT. Excellent idea, Mountain. Armed Minute Men, The militias are crawling all over the place. They still can't tell the difference between a Mexican and a real Indian.

BRONSON. Stupid fucking White Man.

MOUNTAIN. Yeah, stupid fucking White Man…

TOP HAT. Yeah…

BRONSON. Shut your trap, Top Hat. You half-breeds talk too much.

*(***TOP HAT*** quickly produces an Indian ID Card.)*

TOP HAT. I'm one hundreth Apache by blood – read and weep, Bronson! *(to ***CAPTAIN***)* My Indian authenticity card.

SILER. Well, I am not the stupid fucking White Man.

*(Some ***RIDGE MEN*** applaud. ***BRONSON*** ups his game.)*

BRONSON. Stupid fucking White Girl then, shouldn't be out here on the playa with the men…

*(***RIDGE MEN*** quietly snicker. ***SILER*** removes a small handgun from her waste band, the ***MEN*** on the ridge go rigid with a step back.)*

Whoa, little sister…

*(***SILER*** swings around pointing off into the distance and fires.)*

STAR MAN. Holy shit she hit a jack-rabbit in-between the eyes!

MOUNTAIN. That's over a hundred yards away.

BROKE ARROW. Dang.

BRONSON. *(slightly impressed)* That ain't Army issue.

SILER. Walther. Picked it up in Germany, didn't know what I'd find out here.

BRONSON. Krout craftsmanship! Damn fine.

SILER. It's yours.

*(***BRONSON*** slips the weapon in his waist belt and ***SILER*** grabs ***BRONSON*** and has his arm twisted behind him expertly.)*

SILER. *(cont.)* Never ever call me little girl again. Call me a bitch, call me a slut, but not little girl. Girls don't do what I do.

MOUNTAIN. Watch your back, Bronson.

BRONSON. Well, you still can't see the Chief, he's in ceremony, he'll be in the lodge sending up prayers for the next 24 hours. He cannot be interrupted. This Tribe lost its boy – leave us in peace.

SILER. I am carrying an important letter I have to deliver to the Chief.

BRONSON. *(reaching for letter)* Give it to me.

SILER. I cannot do that.

> *(Rifle shots pop in the distance.)*

> *(**SILER**'s knees buckle slightly from the heat, and exhaustion.)*

> *(She bravely maintains her standing position. Thunder in the distance as **RAYMOND BIRDSONG** in combat gear runs across the ridge.)*

> *(As **SILER** regains her composure **BRONSON** quickly motions the ok for **TOP HAT** to allow **CAPTAIN** some water from a fake suede squirt pouch. **SILER** drinks.)*

Oh, that's good.

TOP HAT. Sweetwater.

SILER. Thanks.

> *(**SILER** drinks again.)*

TOP HAT. Only in Bumbfuck…

> *(**SILER** passes the water pouch back.)*

Keep it. Drink it slow – it's laced with *peyote.* Or is it this one? Shoot…

> *(**TOP HAT** juggles the water pouches.)*

Yeah, this one. No, that one. I am certain of it. Drink, White Devil Woman.

SILER. Are you the Chief?

TOP HAT. No. I am not. I'm a Road Scholar from East LA College. I'm in my 27th year there. The Chief *has* allowed me to write the history of the Tribe for Google Earth, except now I got writer's block like a mo-fo.

*(***RIDGE MEN*** *guffaw.)*

So, I'm just another high-plains drifter biker outlaw of the Badlands. To all my relations. Ho. *(slightly wrong)*

SILER. Can you help me get a message to the Chief?

(pulling **SILER** *in close)*

TOP HAT. If I did that, these men could shoot me. Then you. They will. This is certain.

SILER. I'm one of the good guys, man.

TOP HAT. Last time a good guy was here. A White US Army Captain was on *this* reservation, things didn't go so well. For the relatives. History, Captain – it's more than a cable channel. Ho!

SILER. Tell the Chief I bring no diseased blankets for fuck's sake.

TOP HAT. Why are you here? What do you want?

SILER. To find out how Raymond Birdsong got killed.

TOP HAT. I can't take that to the Chief.

SILER. Then tell him, I'm not officially representing the Army, and that what *they* say happened over there may not be what happened.

BRONSON. WE ALREADY KNOW WHAT HAPPENED OVER THERE!

SILER. You stay the fuck away from me! The Army isn't telling you the whole Ray thing.

BRONSON. Fuck the U.S. Army and whatever they're saying about Ray. We don't wanna hear it, he's a hero as far as this Tribe is concerned.

STAR MAN. Ray served his country better than it served him.

MOUNTAIN & BROKE ARROW. Damn right he did.

(He whips out a folded newspaper page and reads:)

BRONSON. Treason investigation continues over the death of New Mexico native Raymond Birdsong. Military Officials suspect PFC Birdsong of sharing intelligence with the enemy. Bullshit!

STAR MAN. You're part of the witch hunt!

SILER. That's not true.

BROKE ARROW. She's a narc!

BRONSON. Get the fuck off my rez.

SILER. Anybody around here know a kid named Suarez?

ALL. *(hushed)* Suarez….

TOP HAT. Suarez? Maybe…

BRONSON. Stand down, Top Hat!

SILER. Your Chief is gonna want to know what I have to say. I was with Ray when he took his last breath for God's sake.

(**SILER** *is breathing shallow, she slightly loses her balance.*)

TOP HAT. Captain? Captain?

SILER. *(calmly)* Whoa…I'm fine.

TOP HAT. Star Man, call for Farmer, tell him to fetch Maria 15. Now!

STAR MAN. *(radio call)* Officer Farmer, north of the water tower. Now!

SILER. I'm not leaving…

BRONSON. Get this White broad outta here now!

TOP HAT. Give her a beat, dude. Let her catch her breath. Altitude maybe. Too many Indians…

SILER. I know the desert…

TOP HAT. Hold up. Captain?

SILER. Oh…

(**SILER** *slowly goes down. As soon as* **CAPTAIN SILER**'s *knee touches dirt:*

ALL FUCKING HELL BREAKS LOOSE.

In a split second, we must be transported to the battle-field of another Desert:

Projections and sounds: Hellfire Missile, shoulder rocket fire – low flying Black Hawk Helicopters. Chaos. Smoke. Muslim Prayer calls and US Military radio calls.

A **WOMAN** *in full Burka with an infant and a small child run across the ridge.* **INDIAN MEN** *scatter. Three* **MEN** *in full combat fatigues enter quickly move up and over the ridge.*

A reservation water tower on the horizon looks like a Mosque tower or oil refinery smoke stack.)

SILER. *(cont.)* Birdsong? Birdsong!?

*(***BIRDSONG** *in full Combat Gear appears on the ridge but only to* **SILER.**

And then he and all of it is gone like a wild desert wind. Reservation restored.

SILER *regains her composure. The* **RIDGE MEN** *have made a half circle around* **SILER.**

A beat up golf cart with BIA logo scraped on the doors of this dusty, beat up, wholly improvised mini cop car of the Badlands signals the arrival of BIA **OFFICER FARMER** *– a by the book lawman of the Rez.)*

CHAPTER 3:
Farmer and Maria 15

*(FARMER and MARIA 15 arrive at the scene. FARMER is
a huge lump of a man in full Indian Cop uniform with
trooper type baseball hat and Daisy BB-Gun. He speaks
on his cop radio PA system.)*

FARMER. Smokey, smokey…

*(MARIA 15 is the Elder Trickster Lady of the Rez. She has
the respect of these Indian men. She has a gold tooth.)*

Okay, what's all the hoopla people?

BRONSON. Farmer, escort this trespasser off my rez. Right
now!

FARMER. Okay. Step aside people.

MARIA 15. Don't you put hands on her!

*(MARIA 15 [QUINCE] b-lines to CAPTAIN SILER with
cool water and a towel from the wings.)*

Out of my way, gangway you big lummox.

(MARIA 15 pushes her way thru the Men.)

Get off your fat asses. Make yourselves useful for fuck's
sake.

*(MARIA is a walking pocket-station of handy items:
Hand bacteria bottle and quickly dons pink dish gloves
like a surgeon.)*

What's going on over here dear.

SILER. I'm fine, really.

MARIA 15. Don't bullshit me, sister. Talk to me.

SILER. Oh man…

MARIA 15. Heat spell. Dehydration. Chew on this Cheat-
grass root. Let me see your tongue.

(MOUNTAIN steps in to offer a big buck knife.)

I don't need that, get away.

(MARIA 15 places her hand on SILER's forehead.)

Hillbilly Hot. You picked the wrong day to come on
the rez.

(**MARIA 15** *hands her a small mason jar with water.*)

MARIA 15. *(cont.)* Drink.

SILER. Corn?

MARIA 15. My people call it maize.

(**MEN** *laugh.*)

Everybody pipe down I can't think.

SILER. *(hazy)* Are you the Chief?

MARIA 15. Are you stoned?

Just call me Maria Quince.

SILER. Maria Quince?

MARIA 15. Maria Fifteen. Maria Quince Gatos, Maria Quince Minutos, I can be anywhere on the rez in fifteen minutes. I can deliver a baby in fifteen minutes. Call me Maria 15 for short.

(**SILER**'s *phone has slipped out of her pocket.*)

SILER. My Blackberry. It died.

MARIA 15. Blackberry? *(sniffs)* Even trade.

SILER. I might need that.

MARIA 15. Not here you don't.

SILER. But I need to get a message to the Chief can you help me?

MARIA 15. You *need* to drink that sweet corn water before your tongue gets all swole. Don't you worry about the Chief, he's got plenty worries and heartbreak right now.

SILER. Is that Ray's tree out there?

MARIA 15. How did you know that?

SILER. He told me about his Cottonwood tree.

MARIA 15. They grow all along the Rio Grande, they die each year but make a come back in spring. Ray will, too. For now, we'll lay him there to rest.

SILER. He won't rest.

BRONSON. You done jawing with the *wasuchi*, Maria?

(**MARIA 15** *ignores his query and talks to* **SILER.**)

MARIA 15. Don't worry about them hard on's, they don't know how to talk to women real good. They can talk to the rocks and the Moon like nothing but you make them plenty nervous.

(*MARIA 15 continues to towel* **SILER**'s *red-hot brow.*)

Us women folk have to stick together out here on the rez. This clay will draw out the heat. Are you on your moon, dear?

SILER. No. Haven't had one in a year.

MARIA 15. You'll get *sangre* in an hour, just wait and see. Very exciting. Best get the Moon Hut built now.

SILER. Is everybody here wise like you?

MARIA 15. No, here comes a dumb Indian now. Farmer!

(*Big* **FARMER** *ambles over.*)

FARMER. Yes, ma'am?

MARIA 15. Grab me some pads from the first aide kit in your copper hoopty.

(**MEN** *on the ridge look away.* **FARMER** *goes to cart.*)

FARMER. Is the Captain on her moon, Maria 15?

MARIA 15. Broadcast it across the reservation, why don't ya.

FARMER. (*grabbing car radio*) Smokey, smokey: Attention Tribal people, the Captain is on her "Lady Time."

MARIA 15. It was a joke, Farmer!

SILER. Must be hard for you to live here.

MARIA. It's okay. God touched this dirt here.

SILER. I'm an atheist.

MARIA. I always wanted to be one of those.

(**TOP HAT** *re-enters on his stingray bike.*)

MARIA. Topper! Get me more red clay and sage pronto.

TOP HAT. Yes, ma'am.

(**TOP HAT** *shoves off on his bike.*)

Look out, Neanderthal.

(**FARMER** *barely avoids* **TOP HAT**.)

FARMER. Half-breed.

TOP HAT. Fat fuck Indian retard. To all my relations. Ho!

> *(offstage crash)*

> *(FARMER moves in with the pad and clip board.)*

FARMER. One emergency pad, please sign for it below.

BRONSON. Mr. Homeland Security, get your ass over here.

> *(FARMER moves on to a disgusted BRONSON.)*

> Pads? Aren't we sensitive.

FARMER. I had to let her on the Rez, Bronson. Lil Ray Ray served with her, she's a real Captain, I saw her Dog-tags and everything.

BRONSON. Why didn't you call me on the radio?

FARMER. She's got rank on me, Bronson and I gotta lot of respect for that wasuchi there.

MARIA. Look here Bronzie, this White girl ain't going nowhere. She got the heat spell real bad. Worse I seen. We're lucky she didn't die out here.

BRONSON. Damn lucky I didn't shoot her.

SILER. Lucky I didn't shoot you.

MARIA. She stay's put.

BRONSON. I gotta get'er outta here before the Chief sees her.

SILER. I'm not leaving til the Chief sees *me*.

BRONSON. All this commotion is gonna interrupt the Man while he's in the lodge.

MARIA. We can't put her out. Not right now. No sir.

BRONSON. I'm not losing my gig over this stubborn Army broad.

MARIA. Anybody tell Dacotah she's here?

BRONSON. Oh Lord no.

STAR MAN. She'll get right in the Captain's face.

SILER. Dacotah? Ray's wife. I need to speak to her…

BRONSON. You ain't talkin' to anybody.

MARIA. Leave her put. I mean it. I'll be her sponsor on the rez.

BRONSON. Rez sponsor? Goddamn it no.

MARIA. I'm the medicine man 'round here and I say she stays put.

BRONSON. And I'm the shot-caller 'round here, Maria.

MARIA. I never liked you, Bronzie.

(BRONSON *growls*. MARIA 15 *growls*.)

Don't get your snake skin panties in a bunch.

BRONSON. I'll be in the yurt making three coffins. One for you…*(pointing)* one for Farmer and one for Top Hat, damn Gringo lovers. Star Man.

STAR MAN. Yes, sir.

MARIA. Farmer?

FARMER. Yes, ma'am?

MARIA. Run over to Dairy Queen and get Captain some grub.

FARMER. Roger that. I'll get you some onion rings. I can't have them on account of my high cholesterol.

(FARMER *leans in close to the* CAPTAIN *and speaks in hushed tones.*)

My daddy was a White Man.

SILER. Thank you.

FARMER. I'm an evangelical Christian.

SILER. Thank you.

FARMER. I'm circumcised like Ray.

SILER. Thank you.

FARMER. Anyway.

BRONSON. Get her outta here before nightfall!

MARIA. Not if I can help it.

FARMER. Smokey, smokey. Back to base, over.

(FARMER *heads out across the stage with his mini-cop/ cart:* RAY BIRDSONG *gives a soft salute to* SILER *from the back bench of the cart.*)

(Clouds begin to move in over the Rez changing slightly the New Mexican light.)

*(**MARIA** crouches down to **SILER** and mixes more red clay with water.)*

SILER. Can you tell me anything about a boy Suarez?

MARIA. Never heard of them. Him.

SILER. There is a Suarez. From this part of New Mexico. He was deployed the same time as us. Different unit. Suarez?

MARIA. I wouldn't say that name again.

SILER. So you do know him?

MARIA. Just another Indian boy from the rez down the road. Another world.

SILER. Ray said his name to me more than once, right at the end. I suspect they had contact.

MARIA. Impossible Captain. We don't talk to those people. Half-breeds. Haven't done so in a hundred winters.

SILER. Why the hell not?

MARIA. Not allowed.

SILER. But there may have been words over there.

MARIA. Don't know nothun bout that, mama.

SILER. Ray's dead and this kid Suarez is AWOL…

MARIA. Lookie here, I got two new hips and a bum knee, and I can't take another war with the Suarez clan.

SILER. A war? With the Suarez clan…

MARIA. They prolly ain't Indian. Nobody's sure what the hell they are. Just cause they here don't make them Injun by blood.

SILER. What does it make 'em?

MARIA. Here goes a little story G: years ago see, long time, centuries even, those damned Conquistadors landed in Morelia, Mexico. 1640 something, in the holds of those filthy ships were Hebrews, the Jews, like slaves, prisoners and servants of the *pinche gachupines* in their fancy clothes and gold crosses…

(High on the ridge a Spanish Monk and Jewish Slave cross.)

MARIA. *(cont.)* This entire area became their secret home. Crypto's, Sephardic's, Coversos. Los Marranos, what I affectionately call: The Christ Killers.

SILER. Jews on the rez?

MARIA. Shitloads of them. They were dark like us, darker than the Hidalgos, so they could hide among us, infiltrate the Tribes like nothing. But our elders would never allow that. That's why they called it Palestine. Just to piss them off more than they already are.

SILER. So the Birdsong Tribe is pure and they hate the Suarez Tribe because they are not?

MARIA. Just how we were taught.

SILER. Payback in the courtyard…

MARIA. Also, they're a thinner people than we are and that pisses *me* off to no end. Then things sort-a died down until…

SUAREZ. Until what?

MARIA. I can't say no more.

SILER. Maria 15.

MARIA. Great Grandmother took up with a Suarez Man and left this rez for that one. She left on the back of the Bootleggers horse wearing a blue dress they said. Oops! I said too much!

SILER. What are you talking about?

(Offstage: Left, left, left right left. Left…)

(Suddenly three ancient VFW World War Two Veterans march proudly across the ridge.)

(Hunched over, these Vet's can barely walk let alone carry a huge flag, one rifle, a bugle and a small PA System that needs to plug into somewhere.)

(The locals call these guys Old Buzzards. They are a physical marvel and have not missed a parade or pancake breakfast in 68 years.)

MARIA. If you Buzzards are here to get Captain off the rez you'll have to go thru me!

B-1. Look out!

(A shot gun blows off and the Buzzards are gone.)

MARIA. Too many damn guns out here. Chief's lost control of his rez is what he done.

SILER. Did you say Ray's Great Grandmother left this rez for a Suarez man?

MARIA. We gotta stop talken about her right now. I ain't afraid of too many things Captain, but if the Chief hears me talking about that slut – we're dead meat for sure's.

(SILER takes the rez in.)

SILER. Okay.

MARIA. Okay.

SILER. It's sad here. Before Ray sad.

MARIA. You're sad.

SILER. Too much sky.

MARIA. Hides them secrets real good.

SILER. The Konar River could be right there…

(A distant military plane can be heard en route to White Plains, SILER perks up in that direction.)

Apache gun ships?

MARIA. No gun ships out here, mama.

SILER. Ever been to Tora Bora?

MARIA. Ray sent you here.

SILER. You think?

MARIA. *(quiet)* Never seen white skin so up close.

SILER. Sorry…

MARIA. It's nice. Mines leathery. I'm worn.

SILER. I'll treat you to a facial after you take me to the Chief.

MARIA. You can be my gringo spirit guide at the Oriental Nail Spa in Albuquerque!

SILER. You don't get off the rez much…

MARIA. I went to Laverne California once. But it looked like hell so I come running back. I like it here but you got to be tough. Our Tribe, Palestine, we're plenty tough.

SILER. Tough men with guns?

MARIA. Home of the Brave.

SILER. Are they always trying to kick women off this place?

MARIA. That's why I'm the Medicine Man.

(distant hawk)

Look here cappie, I may have bought you a little time before you get the boot off the rez but I never had a BFF and I ain't looken for one now sabe?

SILER. Okay…

MARIA. Okay. Take it easy with the pills, mamma. You'll have to sober up if you're hoping to see the Chief!

(MARIA is gone as SILER moves her duffle bag and lays her head back.

Weary – she opens up her journal and removes a military portrait of Ray Birdsong and unfolds a military map of the Kandehar neighborhood.

She picks up the photo of the dead SOLDIER and a photo of Suarez.

BIRDSONG appears in full gear on the ridge.

She places them on the map and tries to imagine the "crime scene.")

SILER. Birdsong enters a courtyard, Birdsong never comes out of a courtyard…

(SILER puts her head back and places Ray Birdsong's military photo on her chest.)

Is Suarez there? Why is he there? To take you out? And who is this Great Granny in blue dress. Fuck. Help me Ray. Help me. I can't figure it out. Don't you dare cry, Captain. There's no crying on the rez.

DACOTAH. Why is my husband on your chest?

(**SILER** *slowly lifts her head.*)

Why is my husbands picture there?

SILER. Excuse me…

CHAPTER 4:
Dacotah

DACOTAH. You're prettier than they said. I'm plain.

SILER. You're Ray's wife, Dacotah.

DACOTAH. Where's my letter? Did you bring my letter?

SILER. It's addressed to the Chief.

DACOTAH. Fuck the Chief.

SILER. I am very sorry for your loss, Mrs. Birdsong.

DACOTAH. *You're* sorry? That's fuckin' hilarious. Nobody here ever said *that* shit to me. Don't know what pisses me off more, you saying it or them not.

(**DACOTAH** *moves closer down the ridge to* **SILER.***)*

I dreamt you. I dreamt you were coming here, you know that? I dreamt those dark military cars speeding up the rez road clouds of dust rising behind them like the devil. And all of it headed right to me and the baby. Dreamed you like Crazy Horse dreamed his battles before he fought them. Maybe I'm a relative.

SILER. What's your baby's name?

DACOTAH. Running at your head with sharp scissors.

(**SILER** *remains silent.*)

Ray should have thought this out better.

SILER. Thought what out better, Dacotah?

DACOTAH. Joining up the damn war without even talking to me. He went to the store to get milk for his daughter and came back all signed up. I'm still waiting for the milk.

SILER. Ray was a brave man.

DACOTAH. That's the fucked up part, right? Married the Chief's son thought I had it made but only got played. Another Indian kid without a baby daddy.

I miss my man. He had good snugg's.

(**DACOTAH** *moves down stage.*)

When they sent me Ray's personal things, the Chief wouldn't even come over to see what it was.

SILER. Anything about a kid named Suarez?

DACOTAH. Nuh uh. He liked you though. He didn't want me to know you were a girl. A girl Captain. That's some funny shit.

SILER. When was the last time you saw your man?

DACOTAH. Here. On the rez. On leave. He was here but he wasn't, Ray didn't want to talk about nothing. He was a ghost almost.

SILER. Was he depressed?

DACOTAH. Are you?

SILER. Was he suicidal?

DACOTAH. Are you?

(**SILER** *says nothing.*)

Ray was moody a bunch but not like that. I know my husband, Captain. We talked. But the last time was different, Ray knew something was coming. He knew. He felt it. He was preparing for something he said.

SILER. Like Crazy Horse.

DACOTAH. Like that.

(**DACOTAH** *then lowers the collar of her shirt just enough to show a piercing wound.*)

Like this.

SILER. Oh God.

(**DACOTAH** *shows a second wound over her other breast.*)

DACOTAH. We pierced our skin under his tree his last night here. He said we needed to do it as an offering so he would have good luck with his important meeting with some Indians over-there.

SILER. Indians in Afghanistan?

DACOTAH. Tribes I mean. Elders, clans…?

(*Distant shouts and echo noise on the playa.*)

When we pierced – we tore the skin on our chests together first, but Ray kept going, I got real scared – I pierced before but not like this.

DACOTAH. *(cont.)* I'm a Sundancer, fool.

(slow and methodical)

But Ray was cutting his arms, his thighs. We were both soaked with blood. I never seen Ray so happy – happy about his vision – he had been chosen he said, and that he was now ready.

SILER. Ready for what?

DACOTAH. Great Grandmother came to him. Then Ray went to the Chief. There was a big fight about some secret thing.

SILER. What secret thing?

DACOTAH. Chief won't say. The Chief never tells his son he loves him, his son never tells his daughter he loves her. The stoic Indian bullshit gene passed on from one silent Indian to another. This place made Ray quiet. I hated that.

SILER. Sounds like my daddy, without the Indian part. Even when I became a Captain in his Army, it wasn't enough. It's never enough.

DACOTAH. Why do it then?

SILER. I don't know. It's in my blood. Why do you stay here?

DACOTAH. Off the rez my daughter has two choices: Dairy Queen or 10th runner up in the Miss Navajo beauty contest...

SILER. Right...

DACOTAH. You hook up with my husband over there or what?

(SILER looks at DACOTAH.)

SILER. I did not hook up with your man, Dacotah.

DACOTAH. You got an Indian thing or what?

SILER. I got an Army thing. Raymond helped me through a real bad time...

DACOTAH. My husband helped you?

SILER. He saved me.

DACOTAH. How?

SILER. I was a girl in need of a tourniquet…

DACOTAH. What the fuck?

SILER. I had a real bad thing with some pills the night they told me my father died – I couldn't get home for my mom – fuck my dad…

(**DACOTAH** *smiles.*)

Ray gets these pills out of me and he kept everything on the down low. Real good.

DACOTAH. Is that Army Handbook stuff?

SILER. Not even, we don't always go by the book. You can't. Not there. You shouldn't here.

DACOTAH. *(soft)* Right…

SILER. Those Red Rocks are amazing.

DACOTAH. I eat those rocks. When I had my baby in my belly I craved them. Ray's Red Rocks are in me. The night we lost Ray, I saw his Jaguar out there, she left a spot of bitch blood and was gone. Like him. *(beat)* I gotta get to my baby.

SILER. You have to know this kid Suarez?

DACOTAH. No.

SILER. I don't believe you, Dacotah.

DACOTAH. So I fucked him in the back of Farmer's cop Car. No biggie.

SILER. You were intimate with Suarez?

DACOTAH. Only once.

SILER. Can you take me to him?

DACOTAH. I don't know where the heck he is.

SILER. He's AWOL, Dacotah.

DACOTAH. Don't surprise me one bit. That boy is hella trouble.

SILER. So Ray and Suarez fought about you?

(**DACOTAH** *points off.*)

DACOTAH. See those crows dive-bombing on that baby hawk up there?

(**SILER** *finds the raptor riding the lower thermals.*)

DACOTAH. *(cont.)* Everybody's got beef on the rez.

(**DACOTAH** *takes a step to leave then looks to* **SILER.**)

Little Sky Birdsong.

SILER. Little Sky?

DACOTAH. My daughter's name.

SILER. Okay.

DACOTAH. Just try to remember Captain, you're not the widow.

(**DACOTAH** *puts the Captain's photo of Ray's photo in her back pocket and exits.*

SILER *goes back to her duffle.*)

CHAPTER 5: Buckets & Bonnets

(TOP HAT enters on his metal horse as FARMER appears on the ridge carrying supplies.)

SILER. Hey could one of you guys give a Captain a lift to the Suarez Reservation?

TOP HAT. I could take you on my hog but we might get scalped.

FARMER. We don't scalp anymore.

TOP HAT. Since when? I didn't get the memo.

SILER. Where's your transport vehicle, Farmer?

FARMER. Broke down.

SILER. What if I have to go to the bathroom? Where's the latrine?

(TOP HAT hands the CAPTAIN a bucket.)

TOP HAT. Welcome to Burning Man.

FARMER. Your bonnet for the cold and your pads.

SILER. Bonnets, buckets and pads. Okay.

FARMER. We should open a bed and breakfast…

TOP HAT. White people hella love a bed and breakfast.

FARMER. What do you know about White people dude?

TOP HAT. I used teach Kabala in Santa Fe, so…I know…

FARMER. Oh yeah…

SILER. What do you know about that Suarez Tribe?

FARMER. We're never supposed to speak on them.

TOP HAT. I go over there all the time.

FARMER. Ooh, I'm telling.

TOP HAT. They're good peeps, their Medicine Man gave me this:

(TOP HAT reveals a Rosary with a Star of David.)

FARMER. A rosary?

TOP HAT. With a Star of David at the end of it.

FARMER. Oh my God!!!

(FARMER cowers behind SILER.)

TOP HAT. C'mon Farmer, we can talk! Nobodies listening.

(**BRONSON & MOUNTAIN** *appear on the ridge.*)

BRONSON. Top Hat!

TOP HAT. Yeah?

BRONSON. I told you not to talk to the White Devil.

TOP HAT. But she was just about to give us back Utah.

BRONSON. One more demerit and you're 86'ed off the rez. Half breed.

TOP HAT. Damn hair-plug Indian.

BRONSON. And you, Farmer. Stop conversing with that Indian widow maker. The Chief is gonna be very disappointed in you.

FARMER. Oh man.

(**TOP HAT** *rides off as* **BRONSON & MOUNTAIN** *exit the ridge.*)

SILER. Harsh. This place is too fucking much.

FARMER. Nobody's happy here. Nobody knows who they are. *(wipes snot)* Do I look Armenian?

(**FARMER** *starts to cry.*)

I miss Ray Ray man. He was special, Captain. Special-special and I don't want you or the Army to say anything bad about him. I don't even care if he was a traitor, Captain. I still love him.

SILER. He wasn't a traitor.

FARMER. He was already chosen to be Chief like his daddy – he was this Tribe's future – Ray was bigger than the Sandia Mountains. Bigger than all of Tijiera Canyon where the Manzanos kneel down to Mother Earth.

(**SILER** *offers the man a green kerchief. He blows.*)

I was the one who encouraged him to join the Army, Suarez, too. I give names to the recruiter at the mall. I loved America since 9/11. Is that weird?

SILER. No, Farmer. You can do that.

FARMER. Don't tell nobody 'kay?

SILER. What can you tell me about Raymond?

FARMER. Tough kid. He was the only member from our Tribe who could stand in Crow Dog's Circle. I tried like hell to baptize for the lord our savior in the irrigation ditch between the two reservations but he didn't go for it.

But the cool thing about Ray Ray is that he had the magic medicine just like his Great Granny.

Once I saw these Crows sitting on the telephone wires – they were on five different wires like the shape of music notes.

(We see a projection of 25 Crows on wires.)

Like a song. Perfect notes on the lines:

*(**FARMER** sings soft: La, la, la, la…)*

That was Ray's Bird Song. Those Crows gonna sing his song even if he cannot. Magic. He had it. Sacred.

SILER. I'm allergic to sacred.

FARMER. Anyway.

(The image goes away. Train Whistle.)

SILER. What is that smell?

FARMER. New Mexico green chili. They're roasting them 10 miles away. In Ray's honor.

SILER. Amazing.

FARMER. Sorry I ate your onion rings. My cholesterol is spiking. Anyway…

*(**FARMER** ambles off as **RAYMOND** appears in an isle out in the audience.)*

SILER. Raymond Birdsong. Magic Man. Did you forget to take your magic into the courtyard that day?

*(**RAYMOND** keeps moving slowly thru the isle.)*

Lot of haters on the rez. A renaissance of them. Nobody will say squat about Suarez. Why did you bring me to this fucked up place? Ray? Raymond…

*(**RAYMOND** is gone. **SILER** lays her head back down.)*

FIGURE. They tell me you were with my son when he died.

CHAPTER 6:
The Chief

(This is the **CHIEF**. *He does not need to speak loud.*

He has a formality to his brown blazer, Levi's, bolo tie and lovely fedora.)

SILER. I was. I was there.

CHIEF. My boy.

SILER. Yes sir.

CHIEF. Ray-Ray.

SILER. *(stiffening to attention-like)* Mr. Birdsong.

CHIEF. Did he lay there in a pool of his own blood? Was he scared? Did his last baby tooth shatter in his mouth…

SILER. *(softly)* He was not scared…

CHIEF. Did he think of this place? Ray from the rez? Did he go fast?

SILER. Not fast enough.

(Silence. Distant wind.)

Chief Birdsong, I cannot possibly express how deeply sorry I am for your loss…

CHIEF. You're trespassing on my rez.

SILER. We need to talk, sir.

CHIEF. *(cutting her off)* I already know why you're here. You lost a man in your command, you feel terrible guilt. I forgive you.

SILER. Thank you, sir.

CHIEF. Now go.

SILER. I can't.

CHIEF. You can. Walk away.

SILER. This letter is for you, Sir. I'm not here for the army. I'm here because I made a promise to a dying soldier that I would deliver it to you personally. It was his last request.

(She hands him the letter – Desert wind.)

SILER. *(cont.)* *(carefully)* You want to know what your boy was thinking, its in there. I think you need to open it. Open it. Go ahead.

*(***CHIEF*** *sniffs the letter and pockets it.)*

Oh c'mon, Chief. Dude. Three deserts in four days, no sleep, I deserve to know what's in there. Don't you think?

CHIEF. I don't want my son a restless spirit left out here on the Rez. I want him up there on the Angel's Crest Highway with his Ancestors.

SILER. Ray's in that courtyard, Chief – in country. He's still there – and I will not move past. I will not leave him there. His letter can tell me something.

CHIEF. No.

SILER. Goddamn. *(She turns out.)* Looks like over there over here. Freaks me the fuck out. No offence.

CHIEF. Ancient lands.

SILER. There's a fuck load of red rocks here.

CHIEF. Those rocks are my relatives. They talk to me.

SILER. Gotta be snakes out there. I fucking hate snakes. Are Chief's afraid of snakes?

CHIEF. I respect their poison.
How well did you know my Ray?

SILER. Officers are not allowed to fraternize with…

CHIEF. How well did you know my boy?

SILER. Raymond Birdsong was the only soldier who never stared at my tits. So that made him very different from the gate.
When he landed in the desert from basic, he had this huge grin on his face, other soldiers were fainting from the heat the dust – the stench of dead animals – not our Ray. He was ready man. He was a talker. Always yapping about how fucked up home was but that he loved it here anyway.
He talked about you, his dad the big Chief, he felt he was chosen.

SILER. *(cont.)* chosen to do something big, something really good over there that he could never do here.

(**CHIEF** *softly kicks dirt.*)

Your son helped me though a real bad stretch. He was the only one I could talk to…

CHIEF. Do you think my son was a traitor?

SILER. No, but why would Ray keep a Koran on his person?

CHIEF. It's a Good Book.

SILER. Maybe, but about six months ago – we were escorting a group of suspected enemy combatants when we heard the call to prayer…

(*Upstage* **BIRDSONG** *leads* **MEN** *across the ridge.*)

Ray allows the enemy to stop and pray in the direction of Mecca.

(*The* **MEN** *stop and bend to their knees to pray.*)

And then he does this Indian thing to the east, west, north…

CHIEF. The Four Directions.

SILER. The entire platoon was pissed *and* scared shitless with that stunt. Allowing prisoners to pray during transport? Extremely dangerous.

During joint maneuvers with Echo Company – on the road between Kandahar and The Helmand Province, it was already a deadly week in Indian Country – sorry – anyway there was this dead dog on the side of the road. The Jarheads ahead of us were laughing and taking target practice with the carcass.

(**BIRDSONG** *crosses with the carcass of the dog.*)

Sure enough, Ray stops the entire convoy to bury the dog facing west so that it wouldn't offend the Pashtun children watching. Rumors went flying. They wrote traitor on his locker. Your son was sympathetic, but he was not that. Not a traitor.

CHIEF. Did you discipline him?

SILER. I didn't report it to upper command. That was my fuck up. His friggen audacity was addictive. It couldn't be shut down but it could piss a lot of Army people off.

CHIEF. Piss'em off enough to hurt him?

SILER. Maybe. All I know is that when the call came over the radio that Birdsong was down – and we don't knew who made that call from that courtyard: a strictly no-go zone surrounded by Taliban – 10 minutes away by foot – I sprinted to your son. He was still there Chief, barely.

I hunched down over him and he's got that god-damned Birdsong grin. *(softly)* Serene little bastard.

(A hard thunderstorm begins in the distance.)

He's looking up at me and he's asking me if *I'm* okay. Wow. Wow. I told him to shut his mouth and he just kept smiling.

His boots filling with blood, armored jacket drenched. He motions me closer with his eyes and whispers in my ear to find him – a Rabbi.

CHIEF. A Rabbi?

SILER. Yes.

CHIEF. *(quiet)* Shit.

SILER. Your son is fighting for his life and he's messing with me. He was running recon way below my radar, he knew I was pissed, hell he could have used me. I wouldn't have run out of that fucking courtyard without Birdsong I can guarantee you that.

CHIEF. You failed my son…

SILER. I helped create your son.

(beat)

Well, there were no Rabbi's in the Afghan Provinces. So Ray walks me thru a quick Rosary: after I screwed that up pretty good Ray's looking down at his inside breast pocket –

*(**SILER** gently touches her the area of her own pocket.)*

SILER. *(cont.)* A secret pocket inside a Kevlar vest you never really want to open – that's where your letter was. Then Ray says:

Suarez. Suarez…

(**CHIEF** *looks down.*)

I told him – You're a very brave man Raymond Bird-song – and then he was gone.

(*Hawk screeches across in the distant playa.*)

Like that. And that is exactly how the final moments of your son's life went. It was a bloody day Chief. A bad and bloody day.

CHIEF. In Indian Country…

SILER. As we say…

CHIEF. When Ray went off the rez…

SILER. Yes. Man. I'm a 34 year-old woman who hovers over mortally wounded American kids. My uniform soaked in them. You ever hold a kid in your arms when he's dying? There is this sound, their last fight, a gasp for air.

They're with you and then they're just gone. So gone. I have not heard your rocks talk Chief, no, but I have heard the sound of *that* silence. And it fucks with me. To no end…

(beat) Man, I need me a drink.

CHIEF. Alcohol is strictly prohibited during ceremony.

SILER. Of course it is.

(*Hawk in the distance – some clanging far off.*)

Help me find Suarez.

CHIEF. And then what?

SILER. Find out if he killed Ray.

CHIEF. It doesn't bring him back. He needs to get on. Take your forensics elsewhere. I need you off my rez in a half hour.

SILER. You should have talked to your son more…

CHIEF. What makes you think I didn't talk to my son? We talked.

SILER. The last time he was here? He said something about a big fight at home...

CHIEF. That was nothing, just a young buck stepping up to the Chief. We all did that...

SILER. It was a big deal to Ray.

CHIEF. No. No.

*(***CHIEF*** *removes his hat and steps down stage.)*

Back in the day. On the Greyhound Bus. When we left LA to come here. Ray was barely three years old but he was already talken real good.

SILER. Los Angeles?

CHIEF. After Pine Ridge, Wounded Knee, after Leonard and the FBI, I drifted. Got lost with a pack of wild Urban Indians. We were sent to the Big City. Skid-row, Bunker Hill and junkies.

SILER. How long were you there?

CHIEF. Too many years that don't add up. Then I got this baby boy strapped on my back like a guitar. I was already old to be a new dad but I knew I had to get Ray out of LA. Barely got on that bus with the baby –
And in the back of that Greyhound, little Ray's looking up at me with those big brown eyes and he says: Dad, your fucking up, we gotta get back to the Rez, back on the Red Road, Dad . You're going to be Chief, Dad. You are the one, Dad. I kicked cold-turkey right there.

SILER. Three years old?

CHIEF. I'm paraphrasing. But he said it, man. He said it...

SILER. *(beat)* That's Ray. Where was his mother?

CHIEF. Nodding off at the Olive Motel in a ghetto called Silverlake. Wearing the squash blossom necklace I gave her...
But on that bus, man we were safe, safe from the freaks and the fed's. Best damn time Ray and me *ever* had. Best time. Only time really. My little Fancy Dancer. We talked then.

SILER. Once?

CHIEF. Once…

    (The **CHIEF** *looks out.)*

Years go bye and you're here, but you're not, you see your kids but you don't. You move on the rez like a shadow cloud. Not asking too many questions.

    *(***CHIEF** *looks at the precious letter one last time.)*

Bronson!

    *(***STAR MAN & MOUNTAIN** *step put.)*

STAR MAN. Bronson went to town I reckon, Chief.

MOUNTAIN. We haven't seen him nowhere's aye.

STAR MAN. It's like he's disappeared or something.

CHIEF. Goddamn, as soon as he steps foot on the rez have him drive the lady to town.

STAR MAN & MOUNTAIN. Yessir.

    (They salute: odd.)

CHIEF. No saluting on the rez.

STAR MAN & MOUNTAIN. Yessir.

    *(***CHIEF** *is gone. The* **MEN** *on the ridge exit as* **FARMER** *and* **TOP HAT** *hustle in.)*

CHAPTER 7:
Pup Tents and Rosary's

FARMER. Maria 15 wants us to pitch this pup tent for you to shelter you from the hungry coyotes.

TOP HAT. And pissed off Indians.

SILER. What about the Chief? He wants me off the rez.

TOP HAT. We're sort of defying the Chief for the Medicine Man while Bronson is off rez.

FARMER. We're going to be in big trouble.

TOP HAT. Thank god for these toxic FEMA tents

(**FARMER & TOPPER** *complete pitching the pup tent.*)

(**FARMER** *places a 99-cent dream catcher on the flap of the tent.*)

FARMER. Wal-mart!

TOP HAT. A ho! Sometimes a 99-cent dream catcher will do, huh Farmer?

(**FARMER** *proudly agrees.* **TOP HAT** *moves in close to* **SILER**.)

Say cappie, did the Chief tell you about Great Granny?

FARMER. Topper!

TOP HAT. C'mon Farmer, it's okay, we can talk!

FARMER. About what?

(**TOP HAT** *shows rosary.*)

TOP HAT. About why we sometimes like a big fat matzo ball in our bowl of menudo?

FARMER. No...

TOP HAT. I seen you put smoke salmon on fry bread brother!

FARMER. Never!

TOP HAT. Who's the Son of Abraham?

FARMER. Isaac?

TOP HAT. Who's the son of Isaac?

FARMER. Jacob?

TOP HAT. And who did Jacob lay with?

FARMER. Rachel?

TOP HAT. Why do we know this Farmer?

FARMER. I don't know I'm from the Eagle Clan.

TOP HAT. Because you might be from both Kimo Slobber. Look at this again. Look!

(**TOP HAT** *holds out the Star of David Rosary again.*)

(**FARMER** *turns out and goes to his knees,* **TOP HAT** *stands over him from behind.*)

A Rosary with the Star of David at the end. Your mother was a devout *Guadalupana* your daddy a white man who ate Kosher! It's okay, man!

FARMER. I want my foreskin back.

TOP HAT. Yes you do!

SILER. And the Girl in the Blue Dress –

TOP HAT. Ray's Great Grandmother…

FARMER. She's long gone.

TOP HAT. That's what we're allowed to know…

FARMER. Enough Topper!

SILER. When this woman left, that's when the feuds started between the Tribes?

TOP HAT. She didn't leave captain…She was kicked off.

FARMER. Final warning, Top Hat! (**FARMER** *draws weapon.*)

TOP HAT. Truth is Captain, we'll never really know the truth. Too much goddamned isolation on this rez. We just found out Dylan went electric.

FARMER. Dylan who?

TOP HAT. What I do know, is that some folks tucked
Away in those hills there, still hide
Passover songs inside Mexican Border
Corridos. Mezuzahs were embedded behind
Virgen Mary statues.

FARMER. Blasphemer!

(**TOP HAT** *cracks open his Piece Book.*)

TOP HAT. Nossir! I've done the field research Farmer. I've seen it. Look Captain, if a family didn't know how to properly advance these Rosary Beads, the whispers and rumors would begin in all the little churches from Chilili to Escabosa: mata Christos, mata Christos… Christ Killers.

Jewish blood spilled on Mew Mexico soil

Look at all the towns all up and down highway 25 dividing the state, given *good* Christian names: Santa Fe, Las Cruces, Belen, that meant Jew don't stop here – Indian keep the fuck going!

FARMER. Jesus, save us.

TOP HAT. I know a weaver from Chimayo, whose fine Navajo rugs ended up in the synagogues *and* mosques in Morocco. Reverse Diaspora. Fuck me! The cacti practically grows in the shapes of menorahs around here.

(**TOP HAT** *holds out his arms like a giant Menorah.*)

FARMER. Top Hat's bullshitting you, Captain. He don't know *nuthun* about the Tribe. He's from a gated community in Calabasas.

TOP HAT. Farmer is correct, I am a carpet bagger, I Have lived on the Calabasas Settlements but I have worked hard for a peaceful two state solution with Oxnard. But look at my hook nose, look at my expressive hand movements – I could be I just don't know!

FARMER. Stop it! Stop it!

TOP HAT. Father. Son. Holy Ghost Dancer…if the bishops, if the cardinals from around here suspected a Tribes authenticity, if they thought you were not pure – you could lose land, your water rights – you could lose your Indian-ness…

FARMER. No more!

TOP HAT. There's your secrets! There's your shame. There's your fear and ignorance wrapped in enough superstition to turn to hate.

FARMER. Stop talking or I will shoot!

(**FARMER** *draws on* **TOP HAT**.)

TOP HAT. You're gonna shoot me, Farmer? My Jesus freak fuck, Brother? But you're Indian enough to remember the Santa Fe Trail. That was a killing floor! The *Hispanos* and *Penitentes* practically remembered the Inquisition with Fondness!

FARMER. Damn Zionist!

TOP HAT. I'm not a Zionist, I'm a humanist who simply wants to lay down these elegant *chingazos* so people will finally know the truth about this Tribe.

(**RAYMOND** *has been watching from the ridge.*)

(**SILER** *sneaks behind and disarms* **FARMER**.)

SILER. What planet are we on?

FARMER/TOP HAT. *(hushed awe)* New Mexico…

TOP HAT. I can't prove any of this Captain: the Tribal Elders don't want to know if they're members of the Original Tribe. But you, you can be Don Juan – you can be Carlos Castaneda! 50 Guadalupanas, 50 Rabbi's 50 Ghost Dancers: Tewa – Yaqui await you: Halelujia… Vision Quest Carnalita.
Vision Quest Captain…

FARMER. Help us…

TOP HAT. *(singing)* Le-chaim!

FARMER. *(hushed awe)* I see Jewish people.

(**TOP HAT** *and* **FARMER** *exit as* **RAY BIRDSONG** *appears on the ridge looking directly at the* **CAPTAIN**.)

SILER. *(quiet)* What is all this Ray? Why are you haunting me? What do you want me to do?

(*She lays the detailed map of the Pashtun courtyard on a technical grid out, military photos and cross checks her journal notes.*

She reaches for her water. There are two water pouches. She grabs them both.)

TOP HAT'S VOICE. This one has peyote, this one doesn't…
go deep Cappie – go deep..

SILER. Fuck it…

(She squirts them both into her mouth.)

Land of Enchantment…

(Sound of birds.

She reaches for her med bottle.

MARIA 15 *sweeps the upper ridge.*

She lays back in her pup tent and closes the flap.

The glow from inside **SILER***'s pup tent grows.)*

CHAPTER 8: Peyote Dream

*(Lights begin to shift in slow but radical ways, **SILER**'s pup tent is glowing. She drinks more.*

*A tall, sweaty, gorgeous **CROW DANCER** appears.*

*The **CHIEF** enters up stage on the ridge far right or left — **DACOTAH** and her infant appear on the other side. The **CHIEF** is burning sage or sweet-grass.)*

DACOTAH. And the Father asked his Son,
What are you doing here son?

And the son said; I am here to steal your
Thunder and your Lightening bolt Father.

*(**DACOTAH** walks away.*

*The **CHIEF** sings a soft song: Heya heya heya....*

Lights change.

***TOP HAT** appears on the ridge and cranks up a*

WW2 AIR RAID SIREN:

***SILER** emerges from the tent — red and yellow clay on her face.*

The Muslim call to Prayer is heard.)

SILER. No code. No rules. No back-up.
No Gods in that courtyard.

*(Distant thunder or gunfire as **BIRDSONG** appears.)*

Trust no one. Believe nothing. We are alone Ray.
Nobody is coming...

(A huge moon emerges low in the sky.)

So much sky. So little of me...

(Everything is changing around her, the atmosphere, she is higher than a kite from the Peyote Water.

A small contained fire pops up

*A **SPANISH MONK** from the Inquisition passes the upper ridge.*

Video Images begin to flicker on the ridge, sky and Pup Tent:

Opium Poppy Bulbs/Shoulder Rocket Launchers

Oil Refinery Smoke Stacks/Mosque Towers

Sound: Arabic wailing and Native American women's.

Wisps of Lonely Radio frequencies: The Mighty 690, Jesus Radio, Hillbilly music and other radio shit that seems to get stuck in places like West Texas, Bakersfield and any reservation anywhere in the South West.

Onstage – **DACOTAH** *appears in White Wedding Dress and bouquet as she wanders around the battle-field looking for Ray.*

TOP HAT *leads* **MOUNTAIN** *and* **BROKE ARROW** *across the ridge doing "Jazz Hands" and singing:)*

TOP HAT. Dreidel Dreidel Dreidel, I made it from red clay…

*(***RAYMOND BIRDSONG** *in Dress Uniform, envelope hat*

SILER *is slowly circling with a large Jewish Monster down center stage:*

A large Cactus Golem walks on stage like an Ed Wood character [A huge Cacti with hands and a Star of David bling bling!!!].)

CACTUS GOLEM. Aaaaahhhh!!!!

SILER. Aaaahhhh!

*(***TOP HAT** *speeds by on his bike warning:)*

TOP HAT. Cactus Golem! Cactus Golem! Run for your lives!

(Bride **DACOTAH** *finds* **RAY** *centerstage, he is dressed in full military combat uniform but all in white:*

They kiss passionately and **DACOTAH** *runs off.*

RAY BIRDSONG *stand just a few feet away from* **SILER.**

We are in the deadly Courtyard with **BIRDSONG.**

We see **BIRDSONG** *give hand signals and he is joined by* **SUAREZ** *– both are un-armed.*

Distant fire fighting.

Two friendly **PASHTUN MEN** *approach* **BIRDSONG &
SUAREZ.**

BIRDSONG & SUAREZ *quickly whip around to the
audience –* **3 MEN** *stand in the theatre's vomitory–*

THREE US SOLDIERS *who arrived to provide backup for
Ray.*

BIRDSONG *raises his hands as in "HALT."*

Two **TALIBAN REBELS** *have followed the* **US SOLDIERS**
to the courtyard – **THE PASHTUN MEN** *panic.*

The **US SOLDIERS** *from the vaum start to shout com-
mands.*

The **TALIBAN MAN** *runs across the ridge – he stops and
fires in the direction of* **BIRDSONG.**

BIRDSONG *is hit –*

He falls to his knees.

Then prone

SUAREZ *takes cover.)*

SILER. Birdsong!

*(***SUAREZ** *drags* **BIRDSONG** *a few feet but runs off.*

*Sniper fire, smoke. Chaos as somebody prays and we hear
part of the radio call that Birdsong is down:)*

Raymond…

*(***SILER** *is distracted by the sight of a* **YOUNG WOMAN**
*wearing a vintage blue dress who walks slowly down
center stage, hands behind her back –*

SILER *turns back to* **BIRDSONG** *but he is gone.*

*The Girl in Blue Dress [***DACOTAH***] stands down center
and slowly brings her hand from around her back – she
holds an old menorah.*

She places it on the desert floor just in front of her tent –

An intense pin spot hits the religious relic.

The **SPANISH MONK** *re-appears – the* **GIRL** *counts Rosary Beads improperly.*

BIRDSONG *covers the* **GIRL** *and then leads her away by the hand.*

A **US SOLDIER** *runs across the ridge:)*

Birdsong is down! Birdsong is down!

(We hear the radio call.

MAJOR GENERAL SILER *– Father of the captian appears:)*

MAJOR GENERAL SILER. Daughter.

SILER. Father? Did we lose something over there? Is it possible for an entire country to lose something?

MAJOR GENERAL SILER. You are an embarrassment to our entire family. You were scared.

SILER. We were all scared, Dad. Dad? Daddy?

(Her "daddy" echo's with something deep: drum.

A passage of time, just before sunrise.

The Rez is completely restored in seconds.

Suddenly she is face to face with a **MAN** *in dirty street clothes. All is very quiet.)*

CHAPTER 8:
A Kid named Suarez

SILER. Birdsong? Raymond?

SUAREZ. Suarez. Captain.

SILER. What the hell?

SUAREZ. What the hell.

SILER. Suarez? You look just like Birdsong.

(**DACOTAH** *picks up Menorah.*)

DACOTAH. What is this?

SILER. I found it in the rocks.

(**DACOTAH** *inspects the object.*)

SILER. Is this what you and Ray fought about?

SUAREZ. We didn't fight.

SILER. Bullshit. What happened over-there, Soldier?

SUAREZ. What happened over-there, Captain?

SILER. Did you kill Raymond Birdsong in that courtyard?

SUAREZ. I was his *back-up* in that courtyard, Captain.

SILER. That's jack and you know it.

DACOTAH. You can talk to her…

SUAREZ. Ray found me over there, he reached out to me, asked if I would go with him to meet some Pashtun Tribal Elders near the market. He said we could be like Indian peacemakers.
This Elder guy knew Ray seemed to me, they respected him for what he done: the dog thing, letting prisoners pray and shit like that.

SILER. Stay in the courtyard.

SUAREZ. We walk in and holyshit, the Pashtun Elders are there…

SILER. How many?

SUAREZ. Five, six. Un-armed. Just like Ray called it.

SILER. Just you, Ray and the sandies?

SUAREZ. And no weapons.

SILER. Ray's call?

SUAREZ. Ray's call. He starts talking to them…

SILER. He's speaking Pashto?

SUAREZ. Yeah. Big Balls Ray you know. The Pashtun dudes are really listening. Ray offers tobacco, small gifts then Ray gives the shot-caller sandie dude an Eagle Feather. They're small talk'n, smoking. Ray gets the Elders to agree to a sit down with a main Taliban negotiator. I couldn't even fucking believe it.

SILER. What was the purpose of the sit-down.

(**SILER** *shakes cob-webs.*)

SUAREZ. Ray didn't translate everything for me but it sounded like trying to stop all the attacks on the FOB and the road back to Bagram.

SILER. *(quiet)* Fucking Ray…

SUAREZ. Ray didn't want any more Americans to die. Or the sandies…

DACOTAH. That's Ray.

SILER. And then what?

SUAREZ. Then three guys from *your* company show up.

SILER. Exactly which three guys?

SUAREZ. A dude named Killer, Ghost Face & Bon Jovi.

SILER. Shit. *(slowly bends down resting on knees)*

SUAREZ. They show up, armed, screaming, freaking out, then a small group of Tallies, three or four of them must have followed our guys there…

SILER. How do you know they were Taliban?

SUAREZ. I just do.

SILER. How can you be certain Suarez?

SUAREZ. Kalashnikov rifles pointed all over Ray's Courtyard.

(*Distant automatic weapon fire through out.*)

Ray's trying hard to plead with our guys – Killer and Bon Jovi wanted to arrest everybody including Ray and me – somebody's weapon goes off – bullets rain in from everywhere, all sides, we're pinned down like a motherfucker.

SUAREZ. *(cont.)* But Ray is calm. Killer and his buds run back to the sector like pussy's. I stood with Ray as long as I could but I had to get out of there. More hostiles were coming in. I begged Ray to come with me – Let's go, let's go.

(We hear an echo of that plea as yelled: "Let's go!)

I begged him to take my revolver but he wouldn't.

SILER. You said no weapons.

SUAREZ. I snuck one in my boot.

SILER. Ray?

SUAREZ. He just stood. Smiling. Talking about his Great Gramma. The Tribes.

SILER. Ray told Killer and them?

SUAREZ. Negative Captain. I did.

SILER. And why would you do that?

SUAREZ. I trusted Ray but I didn't trust the fucking Hadji's, I figured I'd get three of his buddies from his unit to shadow us …

SILER. They were from *my* unit you stupid fucking kid, they were *my men* and they hated Ray.

SUAREZ. I didn't know that Captain, I didn't know a lot, I was following Ray. It was his gig.

SILER. Ray sought you?

SUAREZ. He reached out to me, Captain.

SILER. Why would he do that, they hate you here.

SUAREZ. Ray said we were connected thru that thing. That we were the Chosen Ones, being Indian and stuff, we could do what the White soldiers couldn't.

The Pashtun guys joked about all of us being members of the Lost Tribes of Israel like them.

Ray mad a joke about being from Palestine – we all laughed and then it all went to shit in like three seconds. Fell apart all around Ray. I don't even know who's bullets hit him. He was doing his big Indian peace thing, and I fucked it up.

SUAREZ. But when I got down close to him, he told me…
he told me…

SILER. C'mon, soldier.

SUAREZ. To ask for you. He told me to ask for you.

SILER. Here we are.

SUAREZ. Here we are.

(Distant thunder)

SILER. You gotta come in with me, Suarez. You gotta tell
the truth and turn yourself in or your life is over. Do
you understand me, son?

I can protect you…

(**BRONSON** *steps from the vomitory down on* **SUAREZ.**)

CHAPTER 10:
Suarez Surrounded

BRONSON. Freeze Suarez!

MOUNTAIN. Suarez!

(**FARMER** *steps out with his rifle.*)

FARMER. Suarez is AWOL!

SILER. Put your weapons down!

BRONSON. Step away from the prisoner!

MARIA. He's no prisoner!

(**MARIA** *hits* **BRONSON**'s *rifle from under the barrel causing it to fire up into the sky.*

SILER *draws. The* **CHIEF** *enters.*)

CHIEF. Put those weapons down!

MARIA. They're trying to shoot Suarez!

SILER. Call off your guns, Chief!

CHIEF. What the hell is going on here now? Suarez?

SILER. Dacotah was hiding him.

DACOTAH. He's afraid.

MARIA 15. They're gonna kill him.

FARMER. Just give us the word.

SILER. Your rez is out of control, Chief.

(*Silence. Guns.*)

BRONSON. What do we do boss?

SILER. Chief?

CHIEF. Turn him loose.

BRONSON. He's a fugitive!

CHIEF. Lower your weapons, all of you!

(**BRONSON** *lowers his rifle as* **SUAREZ** *tips his hat to the* **CHIEF** *and runs away*)

CHAPTER 11:
The Letter

(The **CHIEF** *pulls out a letter.)*

CHIEF. I want you all to hear this:

Dear Dad, today is a great day, Please tell my angel Dacotah and the others that if you're reading this, I won't be coming home. I know we never talked much, Dad, but I want you to be proud of me, I can't tell you everything I'm doing here but you'll hear about it real soon. I feel like you over here, a real Chief. Afghanistan is full of Tribes and clan elders. War lords and Chiefs living under occupation – Sound Familiar Chief? LOL.

I will hook up with Suarez from down the road, together we'll talk to the Tribal Elders here, we will show them how to make peace, we'll bring the Tribes together just like me and him coming together over-here.

Suarez is okay, Dad, I don't hate him or anything like that. We just always fought because you taught us to. Just like the Army I guess. Say wassup to the Red Rocks and all the guys.

Tell Farmer there's a big Uzbecki guy here who's just as ugly as he is. If you get the chance give my daughter a big hug and Dacotah all my love. Love your son – Ray Ray.

(He carefully folds the letter.

DACOTAH *walks to the Menorah and picks it up.)*

DACOTAH. Captain Siler found it in the rocks.

(She places it down with some force dead square in front of the **CHIEF**.*)*

(soft) What's the story Morning Glory?

*(***CHIEF** *reaches down and lifts the Menorah: 1000-lbs.)*

DACOTAH. Why is this thing here? Its what you and Ray fought about right? Great Grandmother?

SILER. The Girl in the Blue Dress?

CHIEF. Yes…

SILER. Was she kicked off the rez because she converted?

CHIEF. She never converted.

> *(relief from the Rez Folk)*

Because she already was.

> *(distant thunder)*

Great Grandmother, my Grandmother, was Jewish by blood.

> *(Ridge folk react in quiet awe.)*

TOP HAT. The Tribal Elders hid *that* Menorah to keep the secret.

CHIEF. My Gramma didn't want to hide no more, she wanted to worship as she saw fit, so she went down the road and started her own family with the Bootlegger.

TOP HOT. Cleofis Malaquias de Suarez…

CHIEF. He didn't care what candles she lit.

SILER. Does Great Granny have a name?

TOP HAT. Luciana. Luciana Two Mountains.

SILER. Both Tribes have the same Great Grandmother…

CHIEF. Birdsong Blood. Suarez Blood. Same blood.

MOUNTAIN. Jesus Christ, we're Jewish.

TOP HAT. Mazel Tov.

CHIEF. Ray confronted me about all of it, but I denied it, that's when we got in that real bad fight. Last time I saw my boy.

TOP HAT. *(chants) Guadalupine…*

CHIEF. He was just like his Great Granny, sweet and tough like *pinion.*

TOP HAT. *Tonatzin…*

CHIEF. My son knows who he is.

TOP HAT. *Abrahim…*

CHIEF. Bronson!

BRONSON. Yeah boss?

CHIEF. Drive down the road and invite the entire Suarez Clan to Ray's ceremony.

BRONSON. Chief?

CHIEF. It's what my son wanted most.

BRONSON. We can't do that Chief…

CHIEF. But we will…

(**BRONSON** *heads off.*)

And Bronson! Leave the Bushmaster.

(**BRONSON** *puts down the rifle.*)

CHIEF. Go!

CHAPTER 12:
Ray comes back home to the Rez

(The wooden Coffin of Raymond Birdsong appears on the ridge.

Lute. Drum. Shaker.

MARIA 15 *sings her Navajo mourning song:*

FARMER *says the Hail Mary:*

TOP HAT *begins the Kaddish:*

TOP HAT.
YIT'GADAL V'YIT'KADASH SH'MEI RABA

B'AL'MA DI V'RA KHIR'UTERI

V'YAM'LIKH   MAL'KHUTEI   B'CHAYEIKHON
UV'YOMEIKHON

UV'CHAYEI D'KHOL BEIT YIS'RA'EIL

BA'AGALA UVIZ'MAN KARIV V'IM'RU: AMEIN.

(a lovely "mash up" of intra-tribal funeral songs.

One Anglo-cowboy undertaker named **RUBY RIDGE** *in black Cowboy Hat, boots and black shirt pulls Raymond Birdsong across the upper ridge.*

DACOTAH *walks up to the Ridge: she says something private and kisses Ray.*

DACOTAH *gives* **SILER** *the "okay" and she steps up.)*

SILER. *(soft)* Order. Arms. *(slow-slow salute)*
I gotta walk out of the Courtyard now but I will never forget you Soldier. Promise.
By your leave sir.

(She kisses the box.)

My tourniquet.

(Hushed rez as **SUAREZ** *enters in his army dress greens:)*

SUAREZ. I'm ready to tell the truth about Raymond Bird-song.

SILER. They're gonna come at you hard, Soldier.

SUAREZ. I'm ready. I want my cousin Ray to rest.

SILER. Me too, Suarez. Me too.

CHIEF. Today my son begins his journey.
All secrets on this rez end today.

SILER. Amen.

DACOTAH. You're on the Red Road now Captain.

MOUNTAIN. Word.

SALLY 30/30 / LA MEGADEATH. Word.

CHIEF. Thank you, Captain.
Your marker is good on this Rez.

SILER. Good to go then.

(**SILER** *nods up to* **TOP HAT**. *Distant hawk.*)

CHIEF. What day is it, Top Hat?

(**TOP HAT** *sits near a rock on the upper ridge.*)

TOP HAT. Friday boss.

(*Lights slowly shift down.*)

CHIEF. Go ahead then. Sing Granny's song.

(**TOP HAT** *removes two Friday candles from his satchel.*

BRONSON *steps out reluctant but with matches.*

As **TOP HAT** *lights Granny's Friday Shabbat candles he softly sings:*

The **CHIEF** *looks up to the heavens, offers tobacco:*

ALL SONGS INTER-TWINING NOW.)

From the darkness to the light.

(**TOP HAT** *sings:* Baruch atah Adonai, Eloheinu melech…)

Our Son. Our drop of blood,
Ray's spirit flickers strong like the
Fire Tender's flame.
Dar luz.
Dar luz.
Rest, mijo. Rest. Lay down your arms.

CHIEF. *(cont.)* Lay down your rifles now.

I love you, Ray Ray.

I love you, Son.

(Crow Dog's language:) Mi Taku oyasin…

To *all* my relations.

A-Ho.

TRIBE/SILER. A-Ho.

(**BRONSON** *is the lone hold out as he slowly shakes his head not agreeing with all that he is watching.*

Fade to Black. A final drum beat.)

ALSO BY RICHARD MONTOYA

WATER & POWER

6 m, 1 boy (doubling possible)

**Originally performed by the award-winning Chicano/
Latino performance troupe Culture Clash**

**Winner of the 2006 Ted Schmitt Award presented by the Los Angeles Drama
Critics Circle for the world premiere of an outstanding new play**

A hard working immigrant father wants better for his sons, twins named Water and Power. He wants them to be like Mr. Mullholand – deciding where the water flows in this desert pueblo. From the Mother Ditch in Chinatown, to the arroyos and ravines that would become Dodgers Stadium, L.A. re-invents herself faster than a Hollywood soundstage. History is cemented over and stars fade in a blaze of glory, but Water and Power will always be remembered – all will know how the eastside rolls! Everything the brothers stand for hangs in the balance as they meet in room #13 at the Motel Paradise on the eastern edge of Sunset Boulevard. That's a part of the boulevard you never want to find yourself in on a dark and rainy night. L.A.'s not for everybody…

Water & Power is modern noir. What emerges from the long shadows of a rainy night is as mysterious as what will never see the light of day. Who is the Power behind the Power? How does Water flow in a desert? Who controls the streets, cops, gangs or gangsters in suits and ties? Nothing is concrete in L.A. except the river.

"Fans of Culture Clash's chicano-inflected, spoken-word-erupting performance art needn't worry that they've lost sight of their signature gifts. Montoya's latest piece, a tale of brothers and a morass of local and national corruption, daringly bundles these elements into tragedy…A significant step in an ambitious new direction."
- Los Angeles Times

"*Water & Power* possesses some of the familiar untamed wildness and a good deal of the old Clash comedy. But Montoya's writing here has psychological weight, too. He manages to compress the events of one violent night and its aftermath into an episodic play riddled with a specifically Latin fatalism."
- Anne Marie Welsh, *San Diego Critic*

SAMUELFRENCH.COM

www.ingramcontent.com/pod-product-compliance
Lightning Source LLC
Chambersburg PA
CBHW070415120726
47909CB00005B/1665